# FUNNY BOY MEETS THE DUMBBELL DENTIST FROM DEIMOS (WITH DANGEROUS DENTAL DECAY)

WITHDRAWN

## Dan Gutman

OPEN ROAD
INTEGRATED MEDIA

Copyright © 2012 by Dan Gutman
Illustrations © 2012 by Mike Dietz
Cover design by Mimi Bark

ISBN 978-1-4532-7070-7

Published in 2012 by Open Road Integrated Media
180 Varick Street
New York, NY 10014
www.openroadmedia.com

*Dedicated to Joseph C. Gayetty,*
*the inventor of toilet paper.*

*Look it up if you don't believe me.*

WARNING: IF YOU READ PAGE ONE OF THIS BOOK, YOUR I.Q. WILL DROP ONE POINT. IF YOU READ THE WHOLE BOOK, YOUR I.Q. WILL DROP TO ZERO.

# INTRODUCTION

Ah, hahahahahahahahaha!

Prepare yourself, pathetic Earth creatures. For it is I, Funny Boy, the most amusing alien life form in the universe, who has come to save your butts once again. While you sit there on your bloated behinds playing your video games and eating your Frosted Mini-Wheats (which are so much better than both Mini-Wheats that are unfrosted and Frosted Maxi-Wheats), nogoodniks from outer space have been coming to destroy your sad and useless planet. And the only one willing to lift a finger to stop them has been *me*.

But do I get any thanks for saving your world? No. You don't call. You don't write. You don't text. You don't tweet.

You don't care.

First, if you recall, came the airsick alien from Andromeda. Then there were those bubble-brained barbers from the Big Bang. After that came a bunch of chit-chatting cheeses from Chattanooga. I defeated them all with my incredible arsenal of jokes, puns, wisecracks, toilet humor, and . . . uh . . . umm . . . comic timing.

That's when it occurred to me . . . A . . . B . . . C . . . yes! The aliens were attacking in alphabetical order! Somewhere, out in the expanding confusion

of the universe, alien sleazeballs and dirtbags (or is that sleazebags and dirtballs?) were actually waiting patiently *in line* to attack the Earth!

They may have been mass murderers, but at least they were polite!

Who would be next, I asked myself? They would have to start with the letter D, obviously. The Dominating Doofuses from Denmark? The Devilish Doormen from Delta 8? The Daydreaming Daytona Drivers from DeFuture?

Read on and find out.

Or don't. You can just read this page over and over again if you want to. It's a free country. Or you can go see if there's anything good on TV. (As if!) There are lots of things you could be doing right now that have to be better than reading *this* junk.

But to be honest, you might as well go on reading the book at this point, because we're not giving you your money back.

**NOTE TO READER: If you're looking for a well-written, heartwarming, educational story with a valuable life lesson or a positive message that will help you grow as a person and impress your parents and teachers, guess what? You picked the wrong book! Ha-ha-ha-ha!**

If there's anything in this book that you find personally offensive or in poor taste, consult your doctor immediately and ask about getting a sense of humor transplant.

The story you are about to read has been carefully screened by the Parents Advisory Board to be certain it has no inappropriate language, such as dork, booger, burping, lice, maggots, poop, pee, pus, snot, stupid, vomit, moron, armpit, or fart. If you see any words like those, close your eyes immediately before your brain turns to guacamole. Then alert the authorities, so all copies of this book—digital and otherwise—can be destroyed.

## CHAPTER 1

# THIS IS THE FIRST CHAPTER OF THE BOOK. THAT'S WHY IT'S NUMBER 1. IT PROBABLY THINKS IT'S THE BEST CHAPTER, AND GOES AROUND TELLING ALL THE OTHER CHAPTERS HOW GOOD IT IS. ARROGANT JERK!

Perhaps I should introduce myself.

"Self, I would like you to meet Funny Boy."

Oh, wait. Sorry! Maybe instead of introducing myself to myself (which serves no purpose at all) I should introduce myself to *you*. That would make much more sense.

I, Funny Boy, was born on the planet Crouton,
which is about the size of Uranus. The planet, that
is. Crouton is shaped like a loaf of bread. In fact, my
home planet is made of bread, and is quite tasty when
toasted, with a little butter and strawberry jam. Yum!

Crouton is 160,000 million light years away in the
Magellanic Cloud Galaxy. How far is that? It's so far
away that we don't even have a McDonald's on the
whole planet. That's far!

Thank God for Taco Bell!

In case you're wondering (or even if you're not) I

am nine years old, or 3,287 in Croutonian years. You see, Crouton makes one revolution around the sun every day. My planet spins so fast, the centrifugal force makes it almost impossible to keep anything on a table, which always makes mealtime an adventure. Every time you put a plate on the table, it goes flying off and hits the ceiling. So does the table, for that matter. But we solved that problem. We eat on the ceiling.

But I digress, whatever that means.

When I was a little boy, I made the tragic mistake of shooting a spitball at my brother Bronk. Instead of grounding me, my parents did the opposite—they put me in a rocket ship and sent me to Earth. I considered this a bit of an overreaction, but what do I know about parenting skills?

Fortunately, my parents put my dog Punchline in the rocket with me and aimed it toward the Milky Way, even though I personally prefer Snickers. When Punch and I entered the Earth's atmosphere, we were amazed to discover that Punch could not only talk, but could also sing all the songs from the classic Broadway show *West Side Story*.

Even more remarkable, my sense of humor, which

was already highly developed on Crouton, had become enhanced to the point that it was now a superpower. On Earth, I could effortlessly come up with an endless series of jokes, puns, riddles and one-liners. Like this one . . .

Q: What did one eye say to the other?

A: Between you and me, something smells.

Something about Earth's atmosphere had made me hilarious.

**STOP! TURN BACK! IT'S NOT TOO LATE TO DITCH THIS AND READ THAT BOOK THAT WON THE NEW-BERY AWARD.**

My spaceship crash-landed near San Antonio, Texas, just as Punch was singing "I Feel Pretty." In an amazing stroke of luck, we smashed through the roof of an underwear factory. Tons of Fruit of the Looms cushioned our fall and enabled Punch and me to survive the impact. We also received free underwear for life.

Or I did, anyway. Punch prefers to parade around underwearless. She is, after all, a dog. On Crouton as on Earth, dogs do not wear underwear. But they do wear wristwatches. Why would a dog wear a wristwatch, you ask?

To tell time, of course!

When Punch and I landed in the underwear factory, we were discovered by a kindly underwear inspector named Bob Foster who became my foster father, whether he wanted to or not. He took us home against his will, and we became one big happy family, except for Bob, who wishes we would leave already.

Earth had been very, very good to me, and I wanted to do something to help my adopted planet. But what

could I do? I had nothing except the clothes on my back, and I couldn't exactly take *them* off. If I walked around naked I would get arrested, or have my life made into a reality TV show.

Then it hit me—I would be a force of good and use my super sense of humor to fight evil on my new planet! I would don a cape (well, a yellow-checked tablecloth) and a fake nose and glasses to become a superhero I call . . . wait for it . . . Funny Boy!

**WARNING! THIS BOOK SHOULD NOT BE READ BY PEOPLE WITH BACK PAIN, WOMEN WHO ARE PREGNANT, OR ANYONE WHO HAS A BRAIN.**

## CHAPTER 2

# THE BABY BOOM. WHEN FUNNY BOY ATTEMPTS TO APPREHEND A PERFECTLY INNOCENT PERSON ON THE STREET BECAUSE HE MISTAKENLY ASSUMES SHE'S COMMITTING A CRIME.

Why is "abbreviation" such a *long* word? I think there should be an abbreviation for "abbreviation."

Anyway, it was a lovely sunny Sunday, with a few lazy clouds hanging in the sky. There was a slight breeze, and spring was in the air.

But the weather has absolutely nothing to do with

the story, so there was really no reason to bring it up. Don't you hate when they do that in books?

I was sitting in Bob Foster's house minding my own business and watching some adorable cats play the piano on the Internet. Suddenly I felt a rumbling.

"It must be an earthquake!" I shouted to my dog Punch. "Quick! Let's go hide in the bathtub!"

Somebody once told me that during an earthquake, you're supposed to hide in the bathtub. I think it's because you might get all dirty in the earthquake, so you'll want to take a bath as soon as it's over.

"It's not an earthquake, you dope," Punch told me. "That's your stomach rumbling."

Oh yeah. She was right. I was just hungry. So I went and got some Doritos.

**(This is called foreshadowing, by the way. Later in the story, Funny Boy is going to feel a rumbling again, but it's going to be *real* rumbling, because the Earth will be invaded by some intergalactic nutjobs! Only really high-quality literature has stuff like foreshadowing.)**

Bob Foster wasn't home. He had to work over the weekend, inspecting underwear at the factory. Just so you know, Bob inspects underwear as it comes off the assembly line, *not* underwear that people are wearing. If you try to inspect underwear that people are wearing, they scream and you get thrown in jail.

When Bob inspects underwear, he puts a little slip of paper inside that says INSPECTED BY BOB. So if you ever buy underwear and there's a slip of paper inside that says INSPECTED BY BOB, that means that Bob inspected it. Inspecting underwear is a tough job, but it's a lot easier than cutting out those leg holes.

Anyway, Punch said she wanted to go for a walk. Man, she has to go for a walk *all the time*! I would think that if a dog was smart enough to talk, it should be smart enough to use a toilet like the rest of us.

"Okay, okay," I said. "I'll take you out for a walk. Maybe we can catch some bad guys while we're on the street."

So after I ate a few more Doritos and watched a cat play Beethoven's Ninth Symphony, I put on my Funny Boy costume and we headed for the great outdoors.

You would think that bad guys would be all over the streets, wouldn't you? I mean, on TV the streets are filled with robberies, murders, fires, kidnappings, carjackings, and people shooting guns and committing crimes all the time. But when we got out on the street, it was amazingly quiet and peaceful. The only person I saw was some lady pushing a suspicious-looking frilly basket with wheels.

"Halt!" I shouted to the lady.

"Good morning," she replied. "Lovely day for a walk, isn't it?"

"The weather doesn't interest me," I said. "I am Funny Boy, defender of all that is good in the universe! And you're under arrest!"

"What did I do?" she asked, acting all innocent.

"I have reason to believe you have illegal contraband in that rolly basket," I said. "Come with me. You have the right to remain silent."

"But it's just my baby," she said, picking it up. "See?"

"Put that thing down!" I shouted. "Are you trying to get us all killed? Run, Punch! Run for your life! It's a baby bomb!"

Have you heard about baby bombs? They're bombs made in the shape of babies. Nobody suspects a thing, because babies are so cute. But when you pull the pacifier out of the mouth and you throw the baby bomb at your target, it explodes into a million pieces.

BOOM! A well-made baby bomb can reduce a small building to rubble in seconds.

"It's not a baby bomb," she said. "It's my son, Benjy."

"Oh, *sure* it is," I told her. "Let me see that baby's driver's license."

"He's a *baby!*" she replied. "He doesn't have a driver's license."

"Well, I can see that you're not going to come quietly," I said, "so I need to question you. Tell me, how do you communicate with a fish?"

"What does that have to do with anything?" she asked.

"Just answer the question," I said. "How do you communicate with a fish?"

"Uh . . . you . . . drop it a line?" she guessed.

"Okay, you got lucky on that one," I said. "Well, how about this? Why don't oysters give any of their money to charity?"

"Uh, because they don't have any money?" she guessed.

"No!" I informed her. "Oysters don't give any of their money to charity because they're shellfish. Get it? Shellfish? Selfish?"

"That was worse than the first one," said the lady.

"I'm just getting warmed up," I told her. "Now I'm going to bring out my 'A' material, and you will be unable to resist the awesome superpower of my humor."

"Knock yourself out, Funny Boy."

"A string walks into a bar and asks for a drink," I said. "The bartender says, 'We don't serve strings in here.' So the string walks out, rubs himself against the curb, and ties himself into a knot. Then he walks back into the bar and asks for a drink. The bartender says, 'Aren't you the string that was just here a few minutes ago?' And the string replies, 'No, I'm a frayed knot.' "

Get it—a frayed knot? Afraid not? That's what I call high-quality humor!

"How could a string walk into a bar?" the lady asked.

"It can't!" I told her. "That's part of the reason why it's funny!"

"Look, I'd really love to stay and chat with you," the lady said, "but it's time for Benjy's nap. Say bye bye, Benjy."

"Bye bye," said Benjy. "Gurgle gurgle."

"A baby bomb with a built-in speech synthesizer!" I marveled. "What will they think of next?"

"Just ignore him," said Punch, who had kept her big mouth shut up until this point. "He's an idiot."

The lady looked at Punch.

"Uh, your dog just talked," she told me.

"Yes, she did," I replied, "and do you know what's even more amazing than a talking dog?"

"What?"

"A spelling bee!" I told her. "Get it? Spelling bee?"

"I don't get it."

Clearly, this woman was not that bright and could not appreciate the immense magnitude of my wit.

"I'll let you off with a warning this time," I told her. "But don't even *think* about blowing up one of those speech-synthesized baby bombs in this town. I'm keeping an eye on you, lady."

**SO, ARE YOU ENJOYING THE BOOK SO FAR? IS THERE ANYTHING WE CAN DO FOR YOU? A NICE COOL DRINK? A PILLOW? A NECK MASSAGE? ANYTHING TO MAKE YOUR READING EXPERIENCE MORE PLEASURABLE.**

## CHAPTER 3

# WHERE DO FICTIONAL CHARACTERS GO TO THE BATHROOM?

I, Funny Boy, am a student at the Herby Dunn School in San Antonio, Texas. It was named after some guy named Herby Dunn, who invented the electric spoon. It was a spoon that you plugged into the wall. It didn't have a motor in it, and it didn't do anything, but it was technically an electrical appliance. There was also a solar-powered one that you could use if you found yourself eating lunch in a tanning booth.

My teacher is Mrs. Allison Wonderland. She's really nice, and I can tell that she likes me a lot.

"Take a seat, Funny Boy," said Mrs. Wonderland, when I arrived at school on Monday morning.

"Why?" I asked. "Do you have some extra chairs you're trying to get rid of?"

"Just sit down," said Mrs. Wonderland, "and please, no funny stuff today. I had a rough weekend."

"Of course not," I said as I climbed on the seat and put my head near the floor and my feet on top of the desk.

"Sit *up* please, Funny Boy," said Mrs. Wonderland.

"Well, which is it?" I asked. "Do you want me to sit

up or do you want me to sit down? I could do both, but I might wind up in the hospital. Speaking of which, do you know what usually winds up in a hospital? Watches!"

All the kids looked at me.

"Do you want me to beat him up, Mrs. Wonderland?" asked Sal Monella from the back row.

"No thank you, Sal," she replied. "But thank you for offering to help."

Wow, what a nice guy! On planet Crouton, beating somebody up is what we say when we give somebody a present. At my last birthday party back home, ten kids beat me up. Then we had pizza and cake.

Sal is a huge guy whose fists are bigger than my whole head. He looks like a human meatball. He likes being in fourth grade so much that he's been in it for ten years.

I looked around for Tupper Camembert, who is the love of my life, the most beautiful girl in the world, my reason for living, and the grandchild of Earl Tupper, the inventor of Tupperware.

"Where's Tupper?" I asked the kid sitting next to me.

"She's absent," he replied. "Mrs. Wonderland said Tupper has a dentist appointment."

"Oh no!" I sobbed. "How will I make it through a day without seeing my lovely Tupper?"

**WARNING! THIS BOOK SHOULD NOT BE TAKEN INTERNALLY. READ IT OUTSIDE.**

Allison Wonderland told us to open our social studies books and turn to the chapter on the presidents.

"Who can tell the class the name of the sixteenth president?" asked Mrs. Wonderland.

"Oooooooooh! Oooooooooooooh!" I said, waving my hand in the air. "I know!"

Nobody else had their hand up. What a bunch of dummies we have in our class.

"Anyone?" asked Mrs. Wonderland.

"Meeeeeeeeeeee!" I yelled. "Call on meeeeeeeeeeee!"

"Anyone *else*?" asked Mrs. Wonderland.

None of those dummies put their hand up, so after a long sigh, Mrs. Wonderland called on me.

"The sixteenth president," I said proudly, "was Thornton Dillywad Ping-Pong Nose the Third."

Everybody started cracking up.

"Are you happy, Funny Boy?" asked Mrs. Wonderland. "I called on you, and you said something ridiculous just to draw attention to yourself and make everyone laugh—as usual."

"No I didn't," I said. "Thornton Dillywad Ping-Pong Nose the Third was the sixteenth president of Crouton, my home planet. He was a great man who defended us in the war against the Kluge People, and he also invented microwave popcorn."

Mrs. Wonderland rubbed her forehead, which was a sign that she was really happy.

"I wanted to know the name of the sixteenth president of the *United States*," she said.

"Oh, why didn't you say so?" I said. "That was Abraham Lincoln."

"That's right!" said Mrs. Wonderland. "And does anybody know why Lincoln grew a beard?"

"He wanted to look like that guy on the five dollar bill," I shouted.

"He *was* the guy on the five dollar bill!" said Mrs. Wonderland.

"See?" I said. "It worked!"

Mrs. Wonderland looked out the window for a moment, as if she wanted to jump out of it.

"I'm losing my patience," she said.

"Well, where did you last have it?" I asked. "Did you look under the cushions on the couch? That's where I always find stuff that I've lost."

"Can I beat him up *now*, Mrs. Wonderland?" asked Sal Monella.

"No, Sal," she replied, "but that is awfully thoughtful of you."

Wow, Sal must have really wanted to give me a present. I couldn't wait to see what it was.

"May I go to the bathroom?" Sal asked.

"Certainly," said Mrs. Wonderland.

I knew perfectly well that Sal Monella didn't *really* have to go to the bathroom. He was just saying that to get out of class. Everybody knows that fictional characters don't have to use the bathroom. You never see anybody go to the bathroom in movies or on TV or in books, like this one.

But then it occurred to me that maybe fictional characters go to imaginary bathrooms in their minds. In any case, Sal got up and left the room.

"May I go to the bathroom?" I asked Mrs. Wonderland.

"Why do *you* need to go to the bathroom, Funny Boy?"

"I want to take a bath," I said, which for some reason the rest of the class found amusing.

"Can you be serious for *just one minute*?" asked Mrs. Wonderland. "Come up here and whisper in my ear why you need to go to the bathroom."

I went up to Mrs. Wonderland's desk and whispered in her ear.

"I've never been in a bathroom before," I whispered, "and I've always wanted to know what they look like."

"Go ahead," she said, rubbing her forehead some more. "Stay there as long as you like. Take all day if you want to."

I went down the hall to the boy's bathroom.

I pushed open the door.

I entered the room.

And I was astonished at what I saw in there.

No bath!

How could they have a bathroom with no bath in it? They should call it the "nobathroom." Or the "bath-

lessroom." Or "the room that has sinks and toilets and stalls in it but no bath."

There was just one person in the bathroom—Sal Monella.

"Okay, Funny Boy," Sal said, rubbing his hands together. "Now I finally get to beat you up."

Oh boy! I was going to get a present! And it wasn't even my birthday!

But where was he hiding it? Sal didn't have anything in his hand. He just kept punching one fist into his other hand over and over again. I guess he was hiding the present in his pocket.

"Would you mind if I washed my hands first?" I asked Sal. "I hate getting beaten up when my hands are dirty."

"Go ahead, dork."

On Crouton, "dork" means somebody who is really smart and cool. Wow, I had no idea that Sal wanted to be friends with me. I thought I should make some small talk with him so we could get to know each other better.

"So," I said to Sal as I soaped up my hands, "why do you think sheep don't shrink when it rains?"

"I don't know, dork."

"I mean, wool shrinks," I said. "And sheep grow wool on them. So you would think that a sheep would shrink every time it gets wet."

"You are such a dork, dork," said Sal Monella.

"If sheep shrunk," I said, "we'd have a bunch of tiny little sheep running around. That would be cool! Wouldn't you like to have a little shrunken sheep?"

"No, dork," Sal said.

"You could carry it to school in your backpack," I suggested.

"Will you hurry up and finish washing your hands so I can beat you up?" asked Sal Monella.

Sal and I were really getting along well! I felt a little bit awkward because he was going to give me a present, but I didn't have anything to give him.

"Say, do you want to come over to Bob Foster's house and hang out with me sometime?" I asked Sal. "We could get a sheep and soak it in water to see how much it shrinks. Wouldn't that be fun?"

"That's it!" Sal yelled. "I can't take it anymore!"

I'm not exactly sure what happened next. I bent down to tie my sneaker. Sal must have slipped or something. The next thing I knew, he was on the floor

moaning and holding his head. I think he hit it against the sink.

"*Owwwwwwwwww!*" he said.

At that very moment, the bathroom door opened and Principal Werner came in. He saw Sal Monella on the ground holding his head and me standing over him.

"Funny Boy!" Principal Werner shouted, "Go to my office! Now!"

**WARNING! CONTENTS UNDER PRESSURE. IF YOU READ THIS BOOK, YOUR HEAD WILL EXPLODE.**

## CHAPTER 4

# FUNNY BOY IS GOING TO INVENT A NEW KIND OF CAT FOOD IN THIS CHAPTER. YOU DON'T HAVE TO READ IT. YOU CAN SKIP AHEAD TO THE COOL STUFF THAT HAPPENS LATER ON, WHEN THE ALIEN ATTACKS.

Wow! Principal Werner is a known lunatic who tortures, kills, and eats children. This should be interesting.

I hoped Sal was going to be okay. It just goes to show that you should always be careful not to slip and fall in a bathroom, especially when there's no bath in there. I never did find out what present Sal was going to give

me. He went to the nurse's office so he could have his head X-rayed. They probably won't find anything.

Principal Werner took my elbow and led me down the hall to his office. He closed the door behind us.

"Take a seat," he said. "I mean, sit down. So what do you have to say for yourself, young man?"

"Well, I would just like to say that somebody should invent mouse-flavored cat food," I told him. "Because cats like to chase and eat mice. So wouldn't you think that they would love a cat food that tasted like mouse?"

"I don't care what cats eat!" said Principal Werner. "What I care about is my students, and I will *not* tolerate bullying in this school. We have a zero tolerance policy."

"I thought tolerance was a *good* thing," I told him. "Didn't you tell us yourself that we should be tolerant of all people? So you should have a 100% tolerance policy."

Principal Werner looked at me for a long time.

"Are you putting me on?" he finally asked.

"How could I put you on?" I asked. "You're not clothes."

Principal Werner looked at me for an even longer time. Too long.

"I need to go to the nurse's office to check on Sal Monella," he said. "I'll be back in a few minutes. Then, we're going to talk about suspending you. Do *not* leave this room, Funny Boy."

He left. Wow, I had never been suspended before. It sounded like fun.

I looked around Principal Werner's office. He had paintings of boats and lighthouses all over the walls. He had model ships and captain's hats on his shelves. He even had a coatrack that was made from a wooden paddle. Boy, that guy sure likes boating!

In the shelf by the door, I noticed that Principal

Werner had a long coiled rope. It was like the kind of rope you would use to tie your boat to a dock.

I picked up the rope and started fooling around with it. First I looped it around the legs of my chair. Then I hooked the other end of the rope around the pipe on the ceiling, like a pulley. Then I sat on the chair and pulled the rope so the chair I was sitting on went up to the ceiling. I tied the rope so I was hanging there. It was fun.

That's when Principal Werner came back into the office.

"What are you doing up *there*?" he hollered.

"Well, you said that when you got back you wanted to talk about suspending me," I said. "So I thought I would save you some trouble and suspend myself. Look! No hands!"

"Get out!" he yelled. "Get out of my office!"

**WARNING: IF YOU READ THIS BOOK BACKWARD, IT MAKES NO SENSE AT ALL. AND IF YOU READ IT FORWARD, IT MAKES EVEN LESS SENSE.**

CHAPTER 5

# THIS CHAPTER IS REALLY SHORT. SO IF YOUR MOM OR DAD TELLS YOU THAT YOU CAN'T WATCH TV OR GO OUTSIDE UNTIL YOU READ A CHAPTER IN A BOOK, READ THIS ONE. THAT'LL SHOW 'EM!

By now, you may be getting a little frustrated. I mean, so far there has been nothing in this book about a dumbbell dentist from Deimos. It says right there on the cover that Funny Boy was going to meet the dumb-bell dentist from Deimos. At this point there have been lots of dumbbells, but no dentists, from Deimos or anywhere else. You may feel that you have been deceived. You may ask for your money back.

Well, forget that! You're not getting your money back. I already told you that. We spent your money a long time ago, when we ran out of Q-tips. But what you *will* get—shortly—is the most incredible encounter with an alien yet. A big, disgusting-looking, saliva-dripping alien. Just be patient, okay?

Meanwhile, in Toad Suck, Arkansas, a spaceship came to a soft landing in a grassy field near the Sock Hop Diner. A big, disgusting-looking, saliva-dripping alien was inside.

See? I told you there would be a big, disgusting-looking, saliva-dripping alien!

## CHAPTER 6

**THIS CHAPTER IS PRETTY SHORT TOO. I COULD HAVE PADDED IT OUT WITH A LOT OF USELESS INFORMATION, BUT I WOULD NEVER DO A THING LIKE THAT. (FOR INSTANCE, DID YOU KNOW THAT COWS HAVE FOUR STOMACHS? THAT'S A LOT OF STOMACHS! WHY DO THEY NEED SO MANY STOMACHS? YOU'D THINK ONE STOMACH WOULD BE PLENTY FOR A COW. OR MAYBE TWO, IN CASE THE COW NEEDED A BACKUP STOMACH.)**

When I got home from school, Bob Foster was there.

"How was work at the underwear factory today?" I asked him.

"Same old, same old," he said. "I inspected a thousand elastic waistbands. How was school?"

"Very good," I reported. "I too inspected a thousand elastic waistbands."

(Well, I wasn't about to tell Bob Foster that I had been suspended.)

While Bob Foster was preparing dinner, suddenly I felt a rumbling. At first I thought it was an earthquake that would destroy entire towns and leave thousands of people homeless. But then I realized it was much more serious than that.

I was *hungry!*

It was my stomach rumbling.

"What's to eat?" I asked Bob Foster.

But before he could even answer, the phone rang. Punch picked it up with her paw. She listened for a minute or so, and then she hung up.

"Who was that?" Bob Foster and I asked.

"It was somebody claiming to be Myles Purgallin, the President of the United States," Punch said.

"That *was* President Purgallin!" I yelled.

"Why did you hang up on him?" asked Bob Foster.

"I told him we were about to sit down to eat," said Punch. "We never talk on the phone during dinner."

"You told the president *that*?" asked Bob Foster. "The president is more important than dinner!"

The phone rang again. This time I picked it up.

"Runny Boy, it's *me*," said the voice at the other end of the line. "Myles Purgallin, the President of the United States. Some idiot just hung up on me."

"How do I know for sure that you're the president?" I asked him. "*Anybody* could call up and say they're the president of the United States. Tell me something only the president knows."

"The dot over the letter 'i' is called a tittle," said the president.

"Hmmm," I said, "only the President of the United

States would know that. You must really be the president!"

"Of course I'm the president, you dope!" said Myles Purgallin. "I need to talk to you. It's a matter of national importance."

"Mr. President," I told him, "I am here to serve you. Your wish is my desire. My mission is to help you and my adopted country."

"I need you to come to Washington right away," the president said.

"I'm kinda busy this week," I told him. "Bob Foster wants me to help him paint the front porch. Can I come next week?"

"Aliens have landed!" the president yelled. "Earth could be destroyed by next week!"

Wow! Earth could be destroyed by next week! The front porch was part of Earth. If aliens were coming to destroy Earth, they would certainly destroy the front porch with it. And if they were going to destroy the front porch next week, there was no reason to paint it this week. Hooray! I wouldn't have to paint the front porch! In fact, I wouldn't have to paint the front porch ever, because if Earth was going to be destroyed, there would be no front porches left, and no houses with front porches, and nobody would need a front porch anyway because all life would be destroyed and we'd all be dead and—

"I'll be right over," I told the president.

**ISN'T THIS EXCITING? IF YOU HAVE TO GO TO SCHOOL, GO TO SLEEP, OR GO TO THE BATHROOM RIGHT NOW, DON'T! YOU DON'T WANT TO MISS WHAT HAPPENS IN THE NEXT CHAPTER!**

## CHAPTER 7

# WELL, YOU'RE ABOUT HALFWAY THROUGH THE STORY NOW. IF THIS WAS A FOOTBALL GAME, THERE WOULD BE A HALFTIME SHOW HERE. HEY, WOULDN'T IT BE COOL IF SUDDENLY A MARCH-ING BAND CAME OUT IN THE MIDDLE OF YOUR ROOM RIGHT NOW AND STARTED PLAYING?

Punch, Bob Foster, and I rushed to the airport to catch the next flight to Washington, D.C. Bob Foster got the tickets and we all got on the line to go through security.

"Remember, Funny Boy," Bob Foster warned me,

"no jokes. They don't like it when you make jokes on the security line."

"Who, me?" I said. "You know I would never make jokes for no reason."

We were almost at the front of the line when a lady wearing a uniform told me I needed to take off my shoes.

"Sure," I said, as I took them off. "Is this casual Friday? I didn't realize you folks were so relaxed around here. Do you need me to take off my cape and fake nose and glasses too?"

"Just the shoes, please."

"Speaking of shoes," I asked her, "what type of shoes does a frog wear?"

"I don't know," the lady said.

"Open toad."

I expected her to double over in laughter, but the security lady didn't even smile. I took that as a challenge, and searched my vast memory for another shoe joke I could tell her.

"Knock knock," I said.

"Who's there?"

"Wooden shoe," I said.

"Wooden shoe who?" she asked.

"Wooden shoe like to know?" I told her.

No reaction. Not even a hint of a smile. Oh, this lady was *good*.

"Get out of here before I put you under arrest," she said.

"That reminds me," I said to her, "what did the policeman say to his stomach?"

"What?" the lady asked.

"You're under a vest."

"I said get *out* of here!"

Boy, that lady is good at holding in her laughter! But she has no sole.

Get it? Sole? Shoes?

Forget it.

Meanwhile, in Toad Suck, Arkansas, a hatch opened up in the spaceship that had landed near the Sock Hop Diner. A long ramp was lowered to the ground, and a conveyor belt on the ramp began to move.

One by one, equipment began to emerge from the spaceship and slide down the ramp. A large dental chair. An X-ray machine. A sink. A movable light. Various drills and dental equipment.

(By the way, Toad Suck, Arkansas, is a real place that is thirty-seven miles north of Little Rock. According to legend, it was named "Toad Suck" because the rivermen on the ferry drank so many bottles of booze that they swelled up like toads.)

Ha! And you thought this was just going to be some silly joke book with no educational value.

CHAPTER 8

THIS IS WHERE FUNNY BOY
MEETS WITH THE PRESIDENT
OF THE UNITED STATES. WELL,
NOT THE *REAL* PRESIDENT. JUST
SOME FAKE GUY. THIS WAY, WE
DON'T HAVE TO CHANGE THE
BOOK EVERY TIME THERE'S
A NEW PRESIDENT. PRETTY
SMART, HUH?

Bob Foster, Punch, and I just made the flight in time
and rushed to the White House in Washington. A guard
met us at the gate.

"I have been summoned to vanquish an alien invader who is intent on destroying Earth," I announced.

"Take a hike, sonny boy," the guard said.

"The name is *Funny* Boy," I corrected him, "and I'm not in the mood for hiking or any other type of exercise right now."

After ten minutes of begging and pleading, the guard got on his walkie-talkie. Soon Punch, Bob Foster, and I were ushered into the Oval Office.

The president was sitting at his desk. Well, he was actually sitting *behind* his desk. But that sounds like he was sitting on the floor, hiding behind his desk.

President Myles Purgallin is a tall, short man who

was naked under his clothes. If I was asked to describe his face, I would say he had two eyes, a nose in the middle, and an ear on either side of his head. He was clean-shaven, except for his beard and mustache.

"Dummy Boy," he said, shaking my hand, "it is so good to see you again."

"Why?" I asked. "Were you temporarily blinded?"

President Purgallin opened one of his desk drawers and took out a blue postcard.

"This is why I called you here," he said as he handed me the postcard. It had an Arkansas postmark on it. This is what it said:


### YOU ARE DUE FOR A DENTAL CHECKUP!

**NAME**: PRESIDENT MYLES PURGALLIN

**TIME:** APRIL 20, 2 P.M.

**WHERE:** A GRASSY FIELD NEAR THE SOCK HOP
DINER, TOAD SUCK, ARKANSAS


"April twentieth is tomorrow," I said. "So you have a dentist appointment. What's the big deal?"

He looked at me for a ridiculously long time, mainly so there would be a dramatic pause. Scary music started playing from hidden speakers.

"This postcard is *not* from my dentist!"

**IF YOU READ THIS BOOK AND TELL TEN FRIENDS
TO READ IT, YOU WILL HAVE TEN PEOPLE WHO ARE
NO LONGER YOUR FRIENDS.**

I still didn't get it. Maybe the postcard got sent to
the wrong address. Maybe the dentist was trying to get
new patients. Maybe the president's regular dentist had
run away to join the circus as a fire-eater, and this new
guy was taking his place. It could mean *anything*.

"My secretary called to check on the appointment,"

President Purgallin said. "The guy who picked up the phone said he was an alien, and that he was going to destroy Earth. And get this—his name was . . ."

There was more scary music.

". . . Denny!"

"Denny?" I asked. "Like the fast food chain?"

"The point is that it starts with a D, you dope!" yelled the President. "A . . . B . . . C . . . D! It's the next alien invasion!"

"Why would a dentist want to destroy Earth?" asked Bob Foster.

"Maybe he wants to wear a crown," I suggested. "Get it? Dentist? Crown? Teeth?"

"This is serious, Bunny Boy!" shouted the president.

"Maybe this Denny guy was just in a bad mood," I suggested. "Everybody gets cranky from time to time."

"He wasn't in a bad mood," said the president. "In fact, he was laughing. It was an evil cackling laugh. It was haunting."

"Well, if he had an evil, cackling, haunting laugh, he *must* want to destroy the world," said Punch.

"Yeah," I agreed. "In the movies, villains who want to take over the world always have an evil, cackling, haunting laugh."

"Now you see why I sent for you, Monkey Boy," the president said. "I need you to save the world again."

"It's *Funny* Boy," I corrected him. "Why does it always have to be me? Why don't you just send in the navy to save the world this time?"

"How is the navy going to get to Toad Suck, Arkansas?" asked the president. "There are no oceans there."

"Couldn't you airlift the boats in?" I asked.

"No boats in Arkansas!" the president yelled.

"What about the army?" asked Bob Foster. "Isn't it *their* job to defend the country from bad guys?"

"What would I tell the public?" asked President Purgallin. "I'm sending the United States Army to war against a *dentist*?"

"Good point," said Punch. "Now I see why the people elected you to be the leader of the free world."

"So far, we've been able to keep this alien landing out of the news," said the president. "We said that a Hollywood production company is filming a movie about an alien invasion. As long as people think it's just a movie, nobody will get alarmed. The public just *loves* alien invasion movies. But soon the people will catch on that it's not just a movie. That's why I need you, Sonny Boy. You're our only hope."

"What about Bob Hope?" I asked. "He's a Hope."

"He's dead."

"The alien dentist killed Bob Hope?" I shouted. "Now I'm *really* mad! How do we get to Toad Suck? I'm going in!"

"I'll put you on my private jet," the president said. "Good luck to you, Honey Boy."

"It's *Funny* Boy!" I shouted. "Funny with an F."

"Whatever."

Man, I've saved Earth three times already! You'd think the guy would know my name by now.

Meanwhile, in Toad Suck, Arkansas, a full dental office had been set up in the middle of the grassy field. A powerful electrical generator had been hooked up to the rocket engine to provide power.

Three shadowy figures emerged from the spaceship.

## CHAPTER 9

# OOH, THIS IS WHEN THE STORY STARTS GETTING EXCITING! FUNNY BOY IS ON HIS WAY TO TOAD SUCK, ARKANSAS, TO CONFRONT THE DUMBBELL DENTIST FROM DEIMOS. MOVE TO THE EDGE OF YOUR SEAT! THAT IS, IF YOU'RE SITTING DOWN. IF YOU'RE NOT SITTING DOWN, JUST STAY WHERE YOU ARE.

It was fun riding in the president's private jet. The plane had its own ping-pong table, tetherball court, and cotton candy machine.

Psych! It really didn't have any of those things, but

that would have been cool. We *did* get little bags of pretzels, though.

Bob Foster spent most of the flight sleeping. I went over to sit next to Punch.

"I'm afraid, Punch," I confided.

"You're afraid that the evil alien dentist is going to destroy the Earth?" Punch asked.

"No."

"Then what are you afraid of?" she asked.

"Spiders," I told her.

Punch laughed, as only a dog can. Then she closed her eyes, and leaned back in her seat.

"I'm not worried," she said.

"Why not?" I asked her.

"Because I'm a fictional character," she told me. "I can't get hurt. I can't die. Nothing bad can happen to me because I never existed in the first place. That's how I deal with life's problems. We're *all* fictional, y'know."

"So it's sorta the same reason why fictional characters never go to the bathroom, right?" I asked.

"Exactly."

"How can you be so sure we're fictional?" I asked. "You look pretty real to me."

Punch looked at me.

"A talking dog?" she said, putting her paws behind her head. "Come on. Get real. A few chapters from now, the evil alien is sure to die falling off a cliff into a volcano filled with molten hot lava. Or maybe he'll eat a poisoned burrito. Either way, there will be a happy ending. We'll all live happily ever after. Trust me. That's what always happens in stories."

Punch seemed pretty sure of herself. Maybe she was right. Maybe I was getting all worked up over nothing.

But just to be on the safe side, I used the plane's high-speed Internet connection to grab some killer jokes that I could use against the alien dentist.

I went to funnyjokes.com. I went to funnierjokes .com. I even went to funniestjokes.com. There were a lot of great jokes, and they were all free to use without getting permission or paying royalties or anything!

"What do you think of this one?" I asked Punch. "I heard that nearly all accidents occur within twenty miles from home. So I moved."

"Ugh. Is that even a joke?" Punch asked.

"Okay, how about this one? What did the lawyer name his daughter?"

"What?"

"Sue."

"Those jokes are *terrible*," Punch told me. Now there was a worried look on her face. "If that's the best you can come up with, we're all going to die!"

"I thought you said fictional characters can't die," I said.

But Punch didn't hear me. She had gotten up out of her seat to go use the imaginary bathroom in her mind.

**IF YOU EXPERIENCE DIZZINESS, NAUSEA, OR VOMITING WHILE READING THIS BOOK, THAT'S PRETTY MUCH NORMAL.**

## CHAPTER 10

# THIS IS THE INCREDIBLY TENSE SCENE IN WHICH FUNNY BOY APPROACHES THE SPACESHIP. YOU MAY NEED TO SIT DOWN AND TAKE A DEEP BREATH TO CALM YOUR NERVES AS YOU READ IT.

Finally, we landed at Toad Suck International Airport, which serves the greater Toad Suck metropolitan area. Bob Foster rented a car with a GPS so we could find the location of the alien spaceship.

"Choose any car in the aisle," the man at the rental car place said to Bob Foster.

"Any car?" Bob Foster said. "You cannot be serious!"

Bob Foster chose a 1985 Yugo and took Route 35 out of the airport. Then he merged onto Route 22 and made a left at some other road that doesn't exist but I just made up to make it seem like he drove around for a while.

Suddenly, we spotted something in the distance.

"There it is!" Punch shouted. "The spaceship!"

It was a big, silvery space-shippy-shaped thing that towered over the nearby trees. Watching it, I felt the hair on my arms stand up, and realized something right away—I needed to shave my arms. They are *really* hairy.

"If I don't make it back alive," I said to Bob Foster, "you know what to do, right?"

"Rent out your room and sell your stuff on eBay?" asked Bob Foster.

"No!" I yelled. "You should tell everyone how much I loved my adopted planet. Tell everyone how hard I tried to save it."

"Oh yeah," Bob Foster said. "After that, I'll rent out your room and sell your stuff on eBay."

"That might be hard to do after the Earth is destroyed," Punch noted.

"Good point," said Bob Foster as he pulled off the highway at the exit marked "ALIEN DENTIST: TURN RIGHT HERE."

Bob Foster parked the car about fifty yards from the spaceship so we could walk up to it in slow motion and build suspense.

We got out of the car.

We walked in slow motion toward the spaceship.

I put my left foot forward.

I put my right foot forward.

We built suspense. And I did the hokey-pokey.

As we got closer, I could hear scary music coming from behind some bushes. We passed by, and I saw that there was a full orchestra sitting behind the bushes.

"What are *you* people doing here?" Bob Foster asked the musicians.

"We were hired to play scary music," said the violin player. "It enhances the drama of the story."

"Knock it off, will you?" I told him. "I'm scared enough as it is."

The musicians packed up their instruments and left. We advanced closer to the spaceship. On the ground next to it, we could see a complete replica of a dental office, but with no roof. There were four dental chairs.

Suddenly, the spaceship door slid open with a *whoosh*, the way doors always do in science fiction movies but never in the real world. Why is that? I want a sliding door in my house that goes *whoosh*. Those doors are cool.

Standing before us was . . . the dumbbell dentist from Deimos!

**EXCITING, ISN'T IT? I MAY HAVE TO GO LIE DOWN TO REGAIN MY COMPOSURE.**

## CHAPTER 11

# THIS IS WHERE WE MEET THE INCREDIBLY DISGUSTING ALIEN. YOU MAY WANT TO HAVE A BUCKET OR SOMETHING NEARBY, IN CASE YOU NEED TO THROW UP.

Oh, it was an evil-looking creature. Bob Foster, Punch, and I took a step backward, shocked by what we were seeing. The sight was so awful, so repulsive, so disgusting, that just describing it here would probably make me lose my lunch. I'm not sure I can do it.

You insist?

Well, okay.

First of all, his body was a hulking mass of malodorous fat that spilled over the waistband of his sweatpants like a pot of oatmeal that had been left on the stove too long. His face was terrifying, with four eyes arranged in such a way as to allow him to see in all directions simultaneously. His nose was perfectly normal, except for the fact that it was on the top of his head. His mouth was like a mail slot, with rotted, blackened teeth. It looked like he could smoke four or five cigars simultaneously.

What a hideous sight! This alien made Godzilla look like Brad Pitt. We were all trembling with fear and holding onto one another. But at least I didn't throw up.

"KNEEL BEFORE ME," thundered the beast as it came down the ramp from the spaceship. "FOR I AM . . . DR. DENNY!"

"Denny the dentist?" asked Bob Foster.

"THAT IS CORRECT," the monster said, speaking in all capital letters, as aliens tend to do.

"That's a pretty unusual name for an alien dentist," I pointed out.

"EARTH IS A PRETTY UNUSUAL NAME FOR A PLANET. WHO SENT YOU TO SEE ME?"

"The President of the United States," said Punch.

"SO HE RECEIVED MY CARD, BUT WAS TOO COW-ARDLY TO COME FOR HIS APPOINTMENT. HE SENT YOU IN HIS PLACE."

"That's right," said Bob Foster. "Where did you come from?"

"I COME FROM DEIMOS," Denny said.

**WARNING: SHIELD YOUR EYES OR LOOK AWAY! QUICKLY! IF YOU READ THE NEXT PARAGRAPH, YOU WILL ACTUALLY LEARN SOMETHING.**

Deimos? I had a vague memory of Deimos, because my cousin went to a summer camp there one year. It's a dark, reddish moon, the smaller of the two moons of Mars. It circles Mars every thirty hours.

In Greek, the word Deimos means "panic." That's what we were starting to do. This alien looked mean. Bob Foster looked like he was going to pee in his pants. Punch looked like she was going to pee *without* her pants, because as you know, dogs don't wear pants.

"How is Deimos different from Earth?" asked Bob Foster, so he could distract the alien with small talk and maybe it would just leave quietly, as if it had shown up at a boring party and went home early.

"THERE IS NO AIR ON DEIMOS," Denny said. "AND NO WAFFLES."

"No waffles?" I asked. "How do you survive?"

"WE EAT PANCAKES AND PRETEND THEY ARE WAFFLES."

"Well, I guess if you put enough syrup on them . . ." I said.

"Who cares about that?" asked Punch. "Why did you come here?"

"I COULD NOT FIND A DENTIST ON DEIMOS, AND I HAVE DANGEROUS DENTAL DECAY."

"Maybe if they had air and waffles, there would be more dentists," I suggested. "Because if there are two things that dentists love, they're air and waffles."

"Why don't you just be your own dentist?" asked Bob Foster.

"DID YOU EVER TRY TO LOOK IN YOUR OWN MOUTH?" asked the alien.

"You could use a mirror," suggested Punch.

"WE DON'T HAVE MIRRORS ON DEIMOS!"

"You're lucky," I told the alien. "If I looked like you, I wouldn't want to go anywhere *near* a mirror."

"We can get you a dentist right here on Earth," said Bob Foster. "No problem. Then you can leave us alone and go home. Or we can just give you a mirror."

"NO!" thundered Denny the alien. "IT IS TOO LATE FOR THAT. YOUR PRESIDENT HAS OFFENDED ME! SO I WILL DESTROY THE EARTH!"

"Isn't that a bit of an overreaction?" asked Bob Foster.

"Yeah," I said. "Maybe you should start by destroying a small village, just to see if you like it. Then you can destroy a town, and then gradually work your way up to big cities and entire planets."

"ENOUGH TALK!" said Dr. Denny. "I WILL KILL EARTHLINGS ONE AT A TIME UNTIL THEY ARE ALL GONE."

"Not so fast, Denny!" I shouted. "You leave me no choice but to use my superpower to stop you."

"THAT'S *DR.* DENNY TO YOU," Denny replied. "WHAT SUPERPOWER IS THAT?"

"My superior sense of humor!" I replied. "What do you call a fish with no eyes?"

"WHAT?"

"A fsh," I told him. "Get it? No I?"

"That's *it*?" asked Punch. "*That's* the best joke you can come up with? *That's* your superior sense of humor? Do you realize how desperate we are? This guy is going to destroy the world!"

"Okay, how about this one?" I asked. "How do you make a werewolf stew?"

"HOW?"

"Keep him waiting in line for two hours," I said.

"That's just awful," said Bob Foster.

But I thought I saw the corner of the alien's disgusting, dripping mouth go up a little to form the hint of a smile.

"What did Noah use so he could see in his ark?" I asked quickly.

"WHAT?"

"Floodlights," I told him.

A smile! There was definitely a smile creeping onto his disgusting, malodorous face.

"What are the names of the little rivers that run into the Nile?" I asked.

"I GIVE UP."

"The juveniles!" I said.

"Look!" Punch yelled. "I think he's laughing!"

"I AM NOT!" hollered the alien.

"Who invented fractions?" I asked.

"WHO?"

"Henry the One-Eighth," I told him.

Denny's enormous, malodorous belly was jiggling now. He wiped away the tears from his filthy, sunken eyes. He was having a hard time controlling himself. All I needed was one more joke to put him away.

"This walrus walks into a bar—"

"STOP!" Dr. Denny hollered, "BRING OUT THE HOS-TAGE!"

The door to the spaceship opened once again with a *whoosh*. And standing there was the love of my life, the beautiful Tupper Camembert.

## CHAPTER 12

# OH, YOU GOTTA READ THIS! IT'S ALL ABOUT DR. DENNY AND HIS DIABOLICALLY PREPOSTEROUS PLAN TO DESTROY THE WORLD.

"Tupper!" I shouted.

"Funny Boy!" Tupper shouted.

"Tupper!"

"Funny Boy!"

"Tupper!"

"Funny Boy!"

"Will you two shut up already?" Bob Foster said. "You're annoying."

Tupper was standing there in the spaceship door

wrapped up like a mummy, except for her face, which was covered in tears.

"I TRICKED YOUR LITTLE GIRLFRIEND INTO COMING TO ME FOR A DENTAL APPOINTMENT," said the alien. "DO YOU THINK *THAT'S* FUNNY, FUNNY BOY?"

"Let her go, Dr. Denny!" I shouted. "She never hurt anyone. Well, except for that time at school when she opened the door to her locker and it whacked me in the face."

"That was an accident!" said Tupper, sobbing.

At that moment, on either side of Tupper, two other alien greaseballs emerged. They grabbed her roughly by the arms.

"I WOULD LIKE YOU TO MEET MY DENTAL HYGIENISTS," said Denny. "THEIR NAMES ARE HALITOSIS AND GINGIVITIS."

"GRRRRRRRRRRR," said Halitosis. "KILL!"

"RGGGGGGGGGG," said Gingivitis. "DIE!"

Oh great. Now I would have to deal with *three* of them. They were awful looking, vomit-inducing creatures, too horrible to describe. Just think of the most ugly, disgusting-looking monsters possible, and then imagine something doubly repulsive.

"They don't look very hygienic to me," said Punch.

I tried to make eye contact with Denny's hygienist henchmen, but they each had three eyes, and I didn't know which one to look at. They dragged Tupper down the ramp and over to one of the four dental chairs. Then they strapped her into it tightly. She couldn't move her arms or legs.

"Help!" Tupper shouted. "Do something, Funny Boy!"

"You'll never get away with this, Denny!" I yelled. "Surrender now, and maybe the criminal justice system will go easy on you."

"DON'T MAKE ME LAUGH!"

Well, that sure didn't work. Telling bad guys to surrender *never* works. It's just as well, because it would make for really boring stories if they simply gave up as soon as we asked them to.

"KILL?" asked Halitosis hopefully, holding Tupper by the elbow.

"DIE?" asked Gingivitis.

"NOT YET, BOYS," said Denny. "FIRST I MUST DESCRIBE MY PREPOSTEROUS PLAN TO DESTROY THE WORLD."

"Oh, this I gotta hear," said Punch.

Dr. Denny went over to his giant drill, placing one hand on it, almost lovingly.

"SEE THIS?" he said. "I WILL USE IT TO DRILL A HOLE IN THE EARTH."

"Why?" asked Bob Foster.

"I WILL CUT A PATH DEEPER THAN THE GRAND CANYON," Denny said. "AT SOME POINT, THE EARTH WILL SPLIT IN TWO PIECES AND CRACK OPEN LIKE A PISTACHIO NUT! THEN IT WILL SPIN OFF ITS AXIS AND EVERYONE WILL DIE! AHAHAHAHAHA! DRILL, BABY, DRILL!"

"That's preposterous!" said Bob Foster.

"I KNOW," Denny said. "I ALREADY TOLD YOU IT WAS PREPOSTEROUS."

"Do you have any idea how much pain and suffer-

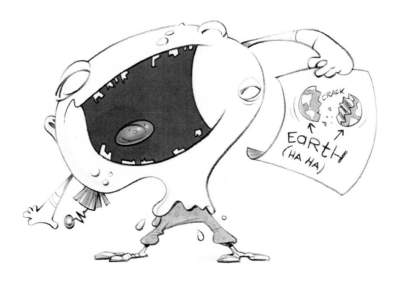

ing that will inflict upon the citizens of Earth?" said Bob Foster. "Have you no sympathy at all?"

"DON'T WORRY," said Denny. "FIRST I WILL DROWN THE PLANET IN NOVOCAINE. THE CITIZENS OF EARTH WON'T FEEL A THING."

"HAHAHAHA!" said Halitosis.

"HAHAHAHA!" said Gingivitis.

"Your preposterous plan will never work," Punch said calmly.

"WHY NOT, DOG GIRL?"

"Because there are only a few more chapters left in this book," Punch said. "These stories always have a happy ending. We're all fictional, you know."

"WE WILL SEE WHO IS FICTIONAL!" shouted Denny. "SEIZE THOSE IDIOTS!"

We tried to make a run for it, but Halitosis and Gingivitis grabbed Punch, Bob Foster, and me. They dragged us over to the dental chairs next to Tupper and strapped us into them.

"I'm sorry, Tupper," I said. "I will always love you."

"I guess our love was not meant to be, Funny Boy," Tupper replied.

"Ugh! Will you two knock it off?" said Punch. "You're going to make me throw up."

Dr. Denny put on a pair of rubber gloves and went over to Tupper's chair. He leaned it all the way back and put one of those heavy vests over Tupper's chest. Then he took some of the dental instruments from a tray and shined a big light on her mouth.

"OPEN WIDE," he commanded.

"No!" she replied.

"HALITOSIS!" Dr. Denny ordered. "KILL FUNNY BOY!"

"KILL!" said Halitosis excitedly.

"Okay, okay!" Tupper yelled. She opened her mouth wide. "Ahhhhhhhhhhhhh . . ."

Dr. Denny looked inside Tupper's mouth.

"HMMMMM," he said. "You have a huge cavity here."

"I do?" asked Tupper.

"YES," said Dr. Denny. "YOUR MOUTH IS A HUGE CAVITY. GINGIVITIS! HAND ME THE LONG METAL STICK WITH THE TINY MIRROR AT THE END."

"No!" Tupper shouted. "Leave me alone!"

"YOU'RE NEXT," Halitosis whispered in my ear. "THE DOCTOR WILL BE WITH *YOU* SHORTLY."

Ugh. He had bad breath. I struggled to get free, but it was no use.

"HAND ME THE SHARP POINTY THING!" Dr. Denny commanded.

"Stop!" screamed Tupper.

"HAND ME THE THING THAT BLOWS AIR ON YOUR TEETH!"

"Help!" shrieked Tupper.

"HAND ME THAT SUCKING THING THAT IS SHAPED LIKE A QUESTION MARK!"

"Hey, don't those instruments have names?" I asked Dr. Denny. "I'll bet you're not even a real dentist. What dental school did you go to, anyway?"

"I WENT TO THE PAINE INSTITUTE," replied Dr. Denny. "THAT IS, PAIN WITH AN E, FOR EXTREME."

"No! Don't!" Tupper shouted. "Funny Boy! Can't you do anything to stop him?"

"Quick, Funny Boy! Tell some of your jokes!" said Bob Foster.

I said the first joke that came to my mind.

"Why don't skeletons fight each other?"

"WHY?" asked Dr. Denny as he worked on Tupper's teeth.

"They don't have the guts," I said.

"THAT IS HORRIBLE," said Dr. Denny. "SPIT."

Tupper spit into a little bowl at the side of the armrest. Then she screamed again, when Dr. Denny forced open her mouth.

"Why did the sheep say 'moo'?" I asked.

"WHY?" asked Dr. Denny.

"It was learning a second language," I said.

"TOTALLY UNFUNNY," said Dr. Denny. "HAND ME THE POKEY THING."

"Your jokes aren't working!" yelled Bob Foster. "What are we going to do now?"

"Help!" Tupper shouted. "Somebody help me!"

Dr. Denny took all the instruments out of Tupper's mouth.

"I HAVE GOOD NEWS FOR YOU," he told her. "YOU NEVER HAVE TO BRUSH YOUR TEETH AGAIN."

"Really?" Tupper said, cheerfully. "That's great!"

"YES," Dr. Denny continued. "THE EARTH WILL BE DESTROYED TONIGHT. SO YOU NEVER HAVE TO BRUSH YOUR TEETH AGAIN."

"Oh no!" we all said.

"KILL?" asked Halitosis hopefully.

"DIE?" asked Gingivitis.

"NOT YET, BOYS," said Dr. Denny. "FIRST I MUST WORK ON NOT FUNNY BOY OVER HERE. OPEN WIDE . . ."

*"Noooooooooooooooooooooooooooo!"*

## CHAPTER 13

# WE'RE GETTING NEAR THE END NOW. WILL FUNNY BOY BE ABLE TO SAVE THE WORLD?

Dr. Denny waddled over to me. He was holding that pointy thing dentists use to scrape stuff off your teeth. I clamped my mouth shut so he couldn't work on me.

"HOLD HIM DOWN, BOYS!" he said to his hygienic henchmen Halitosis and Gingivitis. "NOW OPEN WIDE, UNFUNNY BOY."

"No!" I muttered through gritted teeth.

"OKAY BOYS, KILL THE GIRL!" said Dr. Denny.

"No!" screamed Tupper.

"Okay, okay, I'll open wide!" I yelled. "Leave her alone!"

I opened my mouth. Dr. Denny pointed the light in my eyes and leaned his disgusting, malodorous, dripping face over me.

"HAVE YOU BEEN FLOSSING?" he asked me. "YOU HAVE TERRIBLE HYGIENE."

"Terrible *what*?" I asked.

"HYGIENE."

"My name isn't Gene," I said. "I already told you, I'm Funny Boy."

Dr. Denny failed to appreciate the awesomeness of my hilarity. He was poking around inside my mouth with that pokey thing, and I wasn't liking it at all. I don't even like going to my *regular* dentist. Imagine what it's like to have a dentist who is a big, sweaty alien freak who wants to crack open the Earth like a pistachio nut.

"THIS IS GOING TO PINCH A LITTLE," Dr. Denny said.

"Ahhhhhhhhhhhhhhh! Stop!" I begged.

"Leave him alone!" said Bob Foster.

"YOUR WISDOM TEETH ARE DUMB," Dr. Denny said. "I NEED TO PULL THEM OUT."

"That won't make them any smarter!" I shouted.

"KILL?" asked Halitosis hopefully.

"DIE?" asked Gingivitis.

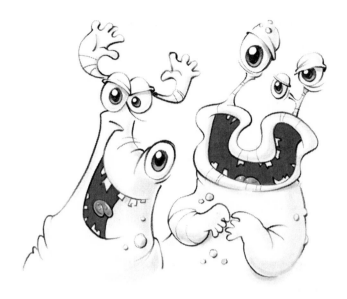

"NOT YET, BOYS," said Dr. Denny as he picked up a tool that looked like a big pliers.

"No!!!!!!!!!!!!!!!!!" I shouted. "Leave my wisdom teeth alone!"

"Tell some jokes, you dope!" Tupper yelled at me. "That's your only weapon."

Oh yeah! The stress of having my wisdom teeth pulled out by an alien dentist had temporarily made me forget about my superpower of humor.

"Do you want to hear two short jokes and a long joke?" I asked Dr. Denny.

"WHATEVER."

"Joke. Joke. Jooooooooooookkkkkkkkkkke," I said.

"PLEASE SHUT UP," said Dr. Denny. "I MUST REMOVE YOUR WISDOM TEETH NOW."

"I will *not* shut up!" I insisted. "What did Geronimo say when he jumped out of the airplane?"

"WHAT?"

"Meeeeeeeeeeeeeeeeeeeeeeeeeeeeee!"

"YOU ARE THE OPPOSITE OF FUNNY," Dr. Denny said, "AND YOUR PATHETIC ATTEMPTS AT HUMOR ARE STARTING TO GET ON MY NERVES."

"Where do polar bears go to vote?" I asked.

"WHERE?"

"The North Poll."

"THAT'S IT!" Dr. Denny said, putting down the pliers. "I WILL PREPARE THE NOVOCAINE! HALITOSIS AND

GINGIVITIS, GO WARM UP THE GIANT DRILL! IT IS TIME TO SPLIT THE EARTH IN HALF!"

The three freaky aliens rushed over to the nearby control panel and started fiddling with a bunch of knobs and buttons.

"Funny Boy!" Tupper whispered. "Do something!"

"What do you want *me* to do?" I replied. "I told my best jokes. He didn't even smile once."

"Don't you know any dental jokes?" asked Bob Foster.

Dental jokes! Of course! Why didn't I think of that earlier? Dr. Denny was a dentist. He would probably find dental jokes to be really funny.

"Yeah," said Punch, "maybe dental jokes would work."

"Woodwork?" I asked. "Who said anything about woodwork?"

"Not *woodwork*," said Punch. "*Would* work. I said dental jokes would work."

"George Washington had wooden teeth," I pointed out.

"What does that have to do with anything?" asked Bob Foster impatiently.

"Punch said woodwork!" I told him.

"I did not!" said Punch. "I said *would* work."

I didn't know what either of them were talking

about. Dr. Denny and his malodorous assistants came back from the control panel. Desperately, I searched my memory for jokes about dentists.

"Why did the dentist go to Venice?" I asked. "To see the root canals."

"HA," said Dr. Denny.

Well, that was a start, anyway. Maybe not a laugh, but it encouraged me.

"Do you know what the dentist of the year wins?" I asked.

"WHAT?"

"A little plaque."

"HA HA," said Dr. Denny.

"I think it's working!" whispered Bob Foster.

"An old man tells his wife that her teeth remind him of the stars," I said. "'Because they twinkle and shine?' the wife asked. 'No,' he said, 'because they come out at night!'"

"HA HA HA," said Dr. Denny.

"He's laughing!" shouted Tupper.

"I AM NOT!" said Dr. Denny.

I didn't care. I was like butter. Because I was on a roll.

"When do most people go to the dentist?" I asked.

"WHEN?"

"Tooth-hurty."

"HA HA HA HA," said Dr. Denny.

"Where does a dentist get gas?" I asked.

"WHERE?"

"At a filling station."

Halitosis and Gingivitis were giggling now too.

"Did you hear about the dentist who went out with a manicurist?" I asked. "They fought tooth and nail."

"HAHAHAHAHAHAHAHA!"

"Why did the holy man refuse novocaine?" I asked.

"WHY?"

"He wanted to transcend dental medication."

Dr. Denny and the hygienic henchmen (that would be a good name for a rock band, by the way) were doubled over in laughter now. It would be impossible for them to drill the Earth in half, because as everyone knows, you can't laugh and commit evil deeds at the same time.

"I CAN'T TAKE IT ANYMORE," said Dr. Denny. "QUICK! GIVE HIM SOME GAS TO SHUT HIM UP."

"What kind of gas?" I asked.

"LAUGHING GAS, OF COURSE!"

**(By the way, if you believe any of this, there's a bridge I'd like to sell you. Really, there is. The bridge is in my grandmother's mouth, but I'll sell it to you for five dollars. She won't mind.)**

# CHAPTER 14

# THIS IS THE BIG SURPRISE ENDING! SHHHHH! DON'T TELL ANYBODY WHAT HAPPENS OR YOU'LL RUIN THE SURPRISE.

Dr. Denny picked up a clear mask and forced it down on my face.

"TURN ON THE GAS!" he ordered.

"No! Stop!" I yelled, trying to fight him off.

"Don't let him do it, Funny Boy!" shouted Tupper.

"HOW WOULD YOU LIKE A TASTE OF YOUR OWN MEDICINE?" said Dr. Denny.

As I inhaled the laughing gas, I felt myself slipping into giggling unconsciousness . . . mind . . . fuzzy . . . haha . . . sleepy . . . funny . . .

With my last ounce of energy, I managed to rip the mask off my mouth, turn it around, and slap it on Dr. Denny's putrid, malodorous face! Right away, he started laughing.

"HAHAHAHAHAHAHAHAHAHA."

"Yes!" shouted Punch. "The laughing gas is working! The tables are turned!"

"What tables?" I asked. "I don't see any tables."

"It's a figure of speech, you dope!" shouted Bob Foster.

Unfortunately, at that moment, Dr. Denny managed to tear the mask off his face. He was still laughing.

"YOUR HUMOR IS TOO STRONG FOR ME, FUNNY BOY!" he shouted. "BUT I EXPECTED THAT, SO I BROUGHT ALONG A BACKUP DENTIST JUST IN CASE. BRING OUT . . . ROBODENT 2000!"

The door to the spaceship opened with another *whoosh* and a huge robot came clanking down the ramp. It was wearing a white dentist's coat and rubber gloves.

"WHERE IS MY PATIENT . . ." asked RoboDent 2000. ". . . DO YOU BRUSH AFTER EVERY MEAL . . . LET ME SEE YOUR GUMS . . ."

RoboDent 2000 rolled over to us and stopped right in front of me.

"A robotic dentist?" asked Bob Foster.

"YES!" said Dr. Denny. "AND HE HAS NO SENSE OF HUMOR, SO HE IS INVULNERABLE TO FUNNY BOY'S STUPID JOKES."

"Oh yeah?" I said. "We'll see about that. What's the messiest sport?"

"WHAT?" asked RoboDent 2000.

"Basketball," I said, "because the players dribble all over the floor."

RoboDent 2000 had no reaction at all.

"Not a sports fan, eh?" I said. "Well, how about this one, big guy? What's the difference between a school teacher and a train?"

"WHAT?" asked RoboDent 2000.

"The teacher tells you to spit out your gum," I told him, "and the train goes 'Chew Chew.'"

Nothing. Dr. Denny was right. The robot appeared to have no sense of humor at all.

"ENOUGH JOKES!" said RoboDent 2000. "I MUST REMOVE YOUR WISDOM TEETH, IN THE MOST PAINFUL WAY POSSIBLE. HAND ME THE PLIERS."

"Nooooooooooooo!" I shouted.

"OPEN WIDE."

"Nooooooooooooo!"

"We're done for!" shouted Bob Foster.

"We're all going to die!" shouted Tupper.

"AHAHAHAHA!" shouted Dr. Denny. "I'VE GOT YOU NOW, FUNNY BOY!"

"Wait!" shouted Punch. "Funny Boy, do you know any robot jokes?"

"RoboDent 2000 has no sense of humor," said Bob Foster. "Even robot jokes will have no effect on him."

"It's worth a try!" said Tupper, with a pleading look on her face.

Desperately, I searched my memory for jokes about robots. There weren't many of them, and they weren't all that funny, but they were all I had.

"Why did the robot mow his lawn?" I asked.

"TO BLEND IN WITH THE HUMANS SO IT COULD INFILTRATE SOCIETY AND ULTIMATELY DESTROY HUMANITY," said RoboDent 2000.

"Wow," I said. "I guess you heard that one already."

"Try another joke, Funny Boy!" begged Tupper.

"How many robots does it take to screw in a light bulb?" I asked.

"NONE," said RoboDent 2000. "WE CAN WORK IN THE DARK."

"Oh, this guy is good," I said.

"Is that all you have?" asked Punch.

"I have just three jokes left," I replied. "What do you get when you cross a robot with a tractor?"

"A TRANS-FARMER," said RoboDent 2000.

"HE KNOWS EVERY ONE OF YOUR STUPID JOKES!" said Dr. Denny. "SOON IT WILL BE ALL OVER FOR YOU, FUNNY BOY!"

"KILL!" said Halitosis gleefully.

"DIE!" hooted Gingivitis.

"Not yet!" I yelled. "I still have two more robot jokes left. Hey RoboDent, did you hear that robots don't have sisters?"

"THEY HAVE TRANSISTORS," RoboDent 2000 responded immediately.

"How did he know *that* one?" I yelled. "*Nobody* knows that one!"

"GIVE UP, FUNNY BOY," said Dr. Denny. "YOU CAN'T BEAT HIM. YOU AND YOUR PATHETIC WORLD ARE FINISHED."

Tupper, Punch, and Bob Foster were sobbing uncontrollably. It was the end of the line. I had just *one* robot joke left. If it didn't work, Dr. Denny would drill a hole in the Earth and split it in half like a giant pistachio nut. The tension was so unbearable that I wasn't even able to make a joke about bears. I gathered up my courage, took a deep breath, and did a few other stalling tactics to build even more suspense.

Okay, finally it was time to let loose the last joke I had.

"What's silver," I asked, "and lays in the grass?"

There was a long pause. RoboDent 2000 didn't move, but it looked like he was thinking.

"He doesn't know the answer!" yelled Tupper.

Smoke started coming out of the robot's ears. It started flailing its arms around.

"I GIVE UP," admitted RoboDent 2000. "WHAT IS SILVER AND LAYS IN THE GRASS?"

"R2 Doo Doo!" I shouted triumphantly.

"HA!" said RoboDent 2000. "HA HA! HAHAHA! HAHAHAHA! HAHAHAHAHA! HAHAHAHAHAHAHAHA-HAHAHAHAHAHAHAHAHAHAHAHAHAHAHAHAHAHAHA!"

"You did it, Funny Boy!" Tupper shouted. "He never heard that one before!"

RoboDent 2000 was laughing uncontrollably, slapping itself on its metallic knees, and wiping away the oil that was dripping from the video cameras that functioned as its eyes.

Dr. Denny, Halitosis, and Gingivitis frantically started scooping up the dental equipment and running to put it back inside their spaceship.

"THE POWER OF FUNNY BOY'S HUMOR IS JUST TOO STRONG!" yelled Dr. Denny. "WE MUST LEAVE EARTH IMMEDIATELY!"

"Put an egg in your shoe and beat it!" I hollered after them. "And don't come back!"

"Hooray!" Tupper shouted. "Hooray for Funny Boy! You are my hero!"

Well, that's the story. Thanks to my incredibly imma-
ture toilet humor, I had driven the evil aliens away. I had
saved the world and made it safe for A lists and B movies, X games and J-walking, iPads and D cups, L trains
and G ratings, C biscuits and E books, T parties and . . .

"See?" said Punch. "I *told* you there would be a
happy ending."

"Some folks just can't take a joke," I said.

**WELL, YOU HAVE WASTED COUNTLESS HOURS
READING THIS NONSENSE WHEN YOU COULD HAVE
USED THAT TIME TO CURE A DISEASE, SOLVE THE
ENERGY CRISIS, OR DO SOMETHING PRODUCTIVE
WITH YOUR LIFE.**

Stay tuned for Funny Boy's *next* amazing and hilarious adventure . . .

*Funny Boy Meets the Evil-Smelling Eggs from Europa (Who Erase Emails)*

# A BIOGRAPHY OF DAN GUTMAN

Dan Gutman was born in a log cabin in Illinois and used to write by candlelight with a piece of chalk on a shovel. Oh, wait a minute, that was Abraham Lincoln. Actually, Dan Gutman grew up in New Jersey and, for some reason, still lives there.

Somehow, Dan survived his bland and uneventful childhood, and then attended Rutgers University, where he majored in psychology for reasons he can't explain. After a few years of graduate studies, he disappointed his mother by moving to New York City to become a starving writer.

In the 1980s, after several penniless years writing untrue newspaper articles, unread magazine articles, and unsold screenplays, Gutman supported himself by writing about video games and selling unnecessary body parts. He edited *Video Games Player* magazine for four years. And, although he knew virtually nothing about computers, he spent the late 1980s writing a syndicated column on the subject.

In 1990, Gutman got the opportunity to write about something that had interested him since childhood: baseball. Beginning with *It Ain't Cheatin' If You Don't Get Caught* (1990), Gutman wrote several nonfiction books about the sport, covering subjects such as the game's greatest scandals and the history of its equipment.

The birth of his son, Sam, inspired Gutman to write for kids, beginning with *Baseball's Biggest Bloopers* (1993). In 1996, Gutman published *The Kid Who Ran for President*, a runaway hit about a twelve-year-old who (duh!) runs for president. He also continued writing about baseball, and the following year published *Honus & Me*, a story about a young boy who finds a rare baseball card that magically takes him back to 1909 to play with Honus Wagner, one of the game's early greats. This title stemmed a series about time-travel encounters with other baseball stars such as

Jackie Robinson, Babe Ruth, and, in *Ted & Me* (2012), Ted Williams.

In his insatiable quest for world domination, Dan also wrote *Miss Daisy Is Crazy* (2004) and launched the My Weird School series, which now spans more than forty books, most recently *Mayor Hubble Is in Trouble!* (2012).

As if he didn't have enough work to do, Gutman published *Mission Unstoppable* (2011), the first adventure novel in the Genius Files series, starring fraternal twins Coke and Pepsi McDonald. There will be six books in the series, in which the twins are terrorized by lunatic assassins while traveling cross-country during their summer vacation. These books are totally inappropriate for children, or anybody else for that matter.

Gutman lives in Haddonfield, New Jersey, with his wife and two children. But please don't stalk him.

Gutman and his sister Lucy in New York in 1956.

A young, stylish Gutman at home in Newark, New Jersey.

Gutman in his Little League uniform in 1968.

Gutman with two babies born in 1990:
the first baseball book he wrote, and his son, Sam.

Gutman in Liverpool, England, at the site of the real Strawberry Field.
"I idolize the Beatles and they inspire all my books," he says.

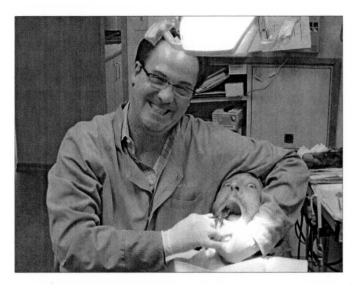

Gutman and his dentist at play (we hope).

Gutman in the midst of adoring fans at
Anderson's Bookshop in Naperville, Illinois.

When he's not writing, Gutman's busy with his favorite hobby, biking.

Gutman and his wife, Nina, at the spot where they met in 1982.

Gutman's wife, Nina, with their children, Sam and Emma.

"After thirty years I made the *New York Times* bestseller list," says Gutman, posing with the second book of the Genius Files, his hit series.

# EBOOKS BY DAN GUTMAN

## FROM OPEN ROAD MEDIA

## Available wherever ebooks are sold

OPEN ROAD
INTEGRATED MEDIA

**Open Road Integrated Media** is a digital publisher and multimedia content company. Open Road creates connections between authors and their audiences by marketing its ebooks through a new proprietary online platform, which uses premium video content and social media.

## Videos, Archival Documents, and New Releases

Sign up for the Open Road Media newsletter and get news delivered straight to your inbox.

Sign up now at
www.openroadmedia.com/newsletters

CPSIA information can be obtained at www.ICGtesting.com
Printed in the USA
BVOW010024161112

305696BV00004B/2/P